S0-AXN-923

# Trouble on
# Black Wind Mountain

*Adapted by* Xu Li
from the novel *Journey to the West*
*Illustrated by* Lu Xinsen

FOREIGN LANGUAGES PRESS   BEIJING

First Edition    1985

Hard Cover: ISBN 0-8351-1365-5
Paperback: ISBN 0-8351-1366-3

Published by the Foreign Languages Press
24 Baiwanzhuang Road, Beijing, China

Distributed by China International Book Trading Corporation
(Guoji Shudian), P.O. Box 399, Beijing, China

*Printed in the People's Republic of China*

The Tang Priest Xuanzang (pronounced Sywanzang in two syllables) and Sun Wukong, the Monkey King, were travelling towards the West. Seeing that the sun was setting, Xuanzang asked Sun Wukong, "Where are we now?" Looking around, Monkey said, "There is a monastery in the valley. Let's go and stay there for the night."

In the monastery, the Tang Priest bowed to the Buddha and saw two young monks come towards him supporting an older one, the Elder of the Golden Pool. He was the abbot of the monastery. Xuanzang hurried to bow to him and asked, "How old are you, Venerable Abbot?" "Two hundred and seventy years old," replied the old monk. "The young people told me you are from the Tang Empire in the East. Welcome."

A young monk brought in three cups of tea. Xuanzang kept saying how wonderful the china was. "But that should be nothing to you gentlemen," said the abbot. "You come from the Heavens and have seen all kinds of fantastic treasures. These things are hardly worthy of your praise. You must have brought some really splendid treasures with you. Could we have a look at them?"

"Yes, the cassock Master has in his bundle is really fantastic," said Sun Wukong. The old monk smiled, "Our Patriarch has seven or eight hundred cassocks I can show you." He ordered the young monks to bring out the cassocks. "That's enough," Monkey said after looking at some embroidered ones. "You should see ours."

Xuanzang drew the Monkey King aside and whispered, "Disciple, never try to compete over wealth. If greedy people see what is precious, they may become envious and do something bad." "Don't worry," replied Monkey, "I'll take care of it." Then he untied the bundle.

When Monkey took out the cassock, the room shone bright with its jewels and Buddhist treasures. All the young monks praised it.

After the abbot saw how splendid the cassock was, he was very jealous. "It was dark just now," he said to the Tang Priest, "and I couldn't see your treasure very clearly. May I ask the monks to take it to my room so I can have a better look at it?" Xuanzang was surprised and grumbled at Sun Wukong. "Don't be afraid of him," grinned Monkey, who handed the cassock to the Elder.

Once the abbot had tricked them into giving him the cassock, he talked with the young monks about how to keep it. "That's easily arranged," said a young monk by the name of Broad Plans. "After they go to sleep we can put wood and grass around their room and set it on fire. The two of them are bound to be killed. Nobody will know how it happened and the cassock will be yours." All the monks agreed with this plan.

But the Monkey King was very clever. When he heard people walking about outside carrying wood in the middle of the night, he wondered what was up. "Could they be bandits trying to murder us?" he thought, and bounded out of bed disguised as a bee to go and have a look.

Monkey saw the monks piling wood and straw around their room, ready to set fire to it. "My master was right," he said to himself with a smile. "But if I killed all of them with my cudgel, the master would be angry with me for murdering them. Instead I think I'll let the old monk have a taste of his own medicine."

Sun Wukong jumped to the Southern Gate of Heaven with one somersault. When he saw the Broad-Visioned Heavenly King there, he told him, "The Tang Priest has met some villains who want to burn him to death. Please lend me your Anti-fire Cover so I can save him. It's urgent." The Heavenly King was unable to refuse and handed the cover to Monkey.

When the Monkey King returned to the monastery, he covered Xuanzang, the white horse and the luggage with the Anti-fire Cover and went to the abbot's room to protect the cassock. Soon the young monks started the fire. Sun Wukong used his magical powers to keep blowing wind at the fire, so that the flames grew bigger and bigger and the monastery became a sea of fire. All the young monks howled and wailed.

Seven miles south of the Guanyin Monastery, in the Black Wind Cave on the Black Wind Mountain, lived a black bear turned monster. When he awoke at midnight and saw an enormous fire, he jumped on a cloud and flew to the monastery to put it out. But he noticed that there was no fire at the back of the monastery where the abbot lived. "Something strange is happening," he muttered to himself.

When the monster rushed into the room he saw something shining very brightly on the table. He opened the bundle and took out a brocade cassock that was a rare treasure of the Buddhist religion. He grabbed the cassock and took it back to his cave.

The big fire didn't stop burning until dawn. The Monkey King quickly returned the Antifire Cover to the Broad-Visioned Heavenly King, thanked him, and came back before the Tang Priest woke up. When Xuanzang woke up and saw that the monastery was gone, he was astonished. "Where are all the buildings?" he asked. Monkey smiled. "What you said would happen actually did happen," he said. "The old monk wanted to burn us to death. So I didn't help put the blaze out. Instead I helped them with some extra wind."

"Sun Wukong," said the Tang Priest angrily, "when a fire starts you should fetch water. How could you blow wind on it?" "The old monk was very wicked," replied Monkey. "If he hadn't started the fire, I wouldn't have blown on it." "The cassock must have been burned up too, then," Xuanzang exclaimed. "No," smiled Sun Wukong. "I kept the abbot's cell safe. Let's take the cassock and leave."

When the Elder of the Golden Pool realized that his monastery had been destroyed and the cassock was nowhere to be found, he was very upset. A young monk came to report, "That Tang Priest didn't die. He's come asking for the cassock." Knowing there would be no escape from Monkey's fury, the abbot smashed his own head against a pillar and died.

Sun Wukong looked everywhere but couldn't find the cassock. Furiously angry with him, the Tang Priest began to recite the Band-tightening Spell. Monkey fell to the ground in great agony, clutching his head and pleading, "Stop, please. I'll see that you get the cassock back." All the young monks begged the Tang Priest to stop too, and he did.

Monkey looked for the cassock again, but could not find it anywhere. He thought for a moment and then asked, "Do you have any monsters around here?" "In the Black Wind Cave of the Black Wind Mountain seven miles south of here lives a Great Black King," said one of the monks. "He's a demon. He often turns himself into a human being and comes here to discuss the Way with us."

"I'm going to have a look," said Monkey. "Take care of my master and the white horse." He leaped up and rode his somersault cloud to the Black Wind Mountain. When they saw that he was an immortal, the young monks were frightened and wished they had not started the fire. They knelt and prayed to Heaven for their lives to be spared.

When Monkey reached the Black Wind Mountain, he saw three monsters — one all black, one in white scholar's robes and one looking like a Taoist priest, Master Emptiness-reached. The black monster smiled and said, "It's my birthday the day after tomorrow. Yesterday I got a beautiful brocade cassock, so I want to invite the two of you to a 'Buddha's Robe Banquet'."

Monkey was so angry he jumped out of his hiding place and shouted, "Monsters, you'd better give that cassock back to me right now." When the three monsters heard this, they tried to flee. The black monster turned into a wind and the Taoist priest rode off on a cloud, so Monkey could only catch the white-robed scholar and kill him with his cudgel.

After rounding several mountain peaks, Sun Wukong found the monster's cave palace. Above the entrance were the words BLACK WIND CAVE. The Monkey King was delighted. He lowered his cloud and shouted, "Open the door!"

The little devil who was guarding the gates opened the door and asked, "Who are you? How dare you come to our cave?" The Monkey King cursed and shouted, "You wicked devil, go and tell that black monster right now to return the cassock to me or else you'll all soon be dead."

The black monster had just made it back to the cave himself. After hearing the little devil's report he thought, "I wonder where this monkey could have come from. He's got a nerve, shouting at my gate." He put on his armour, took up a black spear and strode out.

The black monster shouted to the Monkey King, "How dare you?" Monkey rushed at him with his cudgel in hand and roared, "No more nonsense. Give me back my master's cassock this instant."

"Where did you lose your cassock?" asked the monster. "What makes you think you can find it here?" "I put it in the back room of the Guanyin Monastery," replied Sun Wukong. "You stole it during the fire for your Buddha's Robe Banquet. I know you've got it. If you give it back at once I'll spare your life, but if you say even half a 'no' I'll smash the Black Wind Mountain and trample your cave flat."

The black monster sneered, "Where are you from? What's your name? What magic powers do you have that you dare to boast like that?" Monkey responded, "I am the disciple of His Highness the Patriarch Xuanzang, the younger brother of the Emperor of the Great Tang. My name is Sun Wukong. If I told you my magic powers, you'd be scared to death." The monster sneered again, saying, "You were the Protector of the Horses who wrecked Heaven, weren't you?"

Being called Protector of the Horses made the Monkey King even more furious. This was the very humble job the Jade Emperor had given him in Heaven, and he felt insulted by it. "You vicious monster," he yelled. "You steal the cassock and refuse to return it, and on top of that you insult your betters. Just hold it where you are while I hit you." The monster twisted away from the blow and thrust his own spear at Sun Wukong. After ten rounds neither of them was winning.

At midday the black monster raised his spear to block the cudgel and said, "Sun Wukong, let's take a break. We'll fight again after lunch." Monkey answered, "Forget it. I won't let you have lunch until you give me back my cassock." But the monster fooled him with a wave of his spear, slipped into the cave, and closed the door tightly behind him.

No matter how hard he pushed, the Monkey King couldn't budge the door, so he rode his cloud back to the monastery. "Where is the cassock?" asked the Tang Priest. "I know where it is now," replied Sun Wukong. "It was the monster from the Black Wind Mountain who stole it." He told the story of how he tried to get it back from the monster, and all the monks felt relieved, put their hands together and bowed.

"Don't feel so relieved yet," warned Monkey. "You will only have peace and happiness when I get the cassock back and my master is safely on his way. If you don't keep guard all the time, you'll be sorry." "But during the morning when you were away," Xuanzang told him, "they treated me very well. You can go to get the cassock back without worrying about me."

The Monkey King rode a cloud back to the Black Wind Cave. On his way he saw a small devil coming along the main road from the Black Wind Cave with a wooden box under his arm. "There must be something special in that box," thought Sun Wukong, and he killed the small devil with his cudgel.

When Monkey opened the box and saw that inside it was an invitation from the black monster to the Elder of the Golden Pool to the Buddha's Robe Banquet, he burst out laughing. "So that abbot had been scheming with the black monster. I'll turn myself into his double and trick the devils into giving me the cassock back," he said to himself.

Sun Wukong recited a magical spell that turned him into an exact double of the Elder of the Golden Pool. He strode to the gate of the cave and shouted, "Open the door," imitating the abbot's voice.

The small devil peeped out of the door and hurried to report to the monster, "Your Majesty, the Elder of the Golden Pool has arrived." The monster was astounded. "I just sent the invitation. It can't have reached him yet. Sun Wukong must have asked him to come here for the cassock. Quick, hide it somewhere."

Sun Wukong entered the third gate of the cave and saw the monster, who was wearing a dark green gown. On his head was a soft purple hat and on his feet a pair of deerskin boots. After the monster came down the steps to greet him, Monkey said, "I was on my way to visit you when I ran into the man bringing me your invitation to the Buddha's Robe Banquet. I hurried over to take a look at your cassock."

The black monster laughed and said, "My cassock used to belong to the Tang Priest who has been staying with you. You must have seen it already." "It was dark last night and I couldn't see it very clearly," replied Sun Wukong, "and later, because of the fire and confusion, I couldn't find it anywhere. When I heard that Your Majesty has got hold of it, I came over to have a look."

Before Sun Wukong finished, a small devil on patrol rushed in and announced, "Your Majesty, a terrible thing has happened. Sun Wukong has killed the brother who was taking the invitation card, disguised himself as the Elder of the Golden Pool and come here to trick the cassock out of you." At this the black monster threw aside his gown and thrust his spear at the Monkey King. Monkey changed back to himself, took the cudgel out from behind his ear, and hit back.

The Monkey King and the black monster fought from the top of the mountain to the top of a cloud. When the sun began to set they were still fighting, and neither was winning. "Sun Wukong, it's late now," cried the monster. "Go away and come back early tomorrow and then we'll see which of us is the winner." Monkey didn't want him to leave, but when he hit at the monster, who changed into a puff of wind and blew back into the cave.

Sun Wukong was afraid that his master might be worried about him, so he went back to the monastery. When the Tang Priest saw him returning empty-handed, he asked, "Which of you was better, you or he?" Sun Wukong replied, "I'm not much better than he is, so we stayed pretty evenly matched. But don't worry, I have my ways getting the cassock back."

Early the next morning, just as Monkey was about to slip out, the Tang Priest grabbed him and asked, "Where are you going?" "I've been thinking," replied Sun Wukong. "This is the Bodhisattva's monastery and all the monks here worship her. How could she let a monster live so close by? I'm going to ask her to get the cassock back." Sun Wukong said goodbye to his master and flew straight to the Southern Sea on a cloud.

In an instant, the Monkey King had reached the vast waves of the Southern Sea and the towering peaks and clouds of Guanyin's magic island. While he was looking around, a god stepped forward to greet him and said, "I thought you were escorting the Tang Priest to the West to fetch the true scriptures. What are you doing here?" "I had some trouble on the way," answered Sun Wukong, "so I came here to see the Bodhisattva. Please tell her I'm here."

The Bodhisattva listened to Sun Wukong's story and told him off. "You really have got a cheek, asking me to get the cassock for you. You were showing off the treasure, you blew a wind that burned down my monastery, and now you have the nerve to try making trouble here." Monkey hastily bowed to her and begged her to help him against the monster of the Black Wind Cave.

"All right then, for the sake of the Tang Priest I'll go with you," she agreed. Monkey thanked her again and again and rode a cloud back to the Black Wind Mountain together with the Bodhisattva.

On their way they encountered the Taoist priest, Master Emptiness-reached. He was carrying a glass tray on which were two pills that could make people live for ever. As soon as Sun Wukong saw him, he struck him on the head with his cudgel and killed him. "Why did you have to kill him?" objected the Bodhisattva. "He did you no harm." "I saw him yesterday," explained the Monkey King. "He's a friend of that black monster. He was coming to celebrate the black monster's birthday."

"I have an idea," suggested Sun Wukong to the Bodhisattva. "Why don't you turn into this Master Emptiness-reached? I'll eat one of those pills and turn myself into a pill bigger than the other one. You give the big pill to the monster to eat. Then if he refuses to hand over the cassock I can make trouble in his stomach." The Bodhisattva nodded in agreement.

In a breath of clear wind the Bodhisattva became the Taoist priest and the Monkey King became a big pill of long life. As the Bodhisattva walked towards the cave with the glass tray in her hands, she saw that the cave was set in beautiful surroundings. "Hmm, this monster must have an ounce of faith," she thought and felt sorry for him.

When the monster heard that the Taoist priest had arrived, he came out to greet him. The two sat down together and the Bodhisattva congratulated him. "This humble priest has two pills of immortality to offer you and he wishes Your Majesty a thousand years of life," she said, handing the black monster the larger pill, which rolled down his throat by itself.

At once Sun Wukong began to jump about in the monster's stomach. The pain was more than the black monster could stand. The Bodhisattva turned back into herself and took the cassock from him. Only then did the Monkey King come out through the monster's nostrils.

The Bodhisattva said to the monster, "You beast, will you be a good Buddhist now?" "With all my heart," replied the black monster. "Please spare my life." But Sun Wukong had raised his cudgel and was about to hit him when the Bodhisattva stopped him, "Don't kill him — I need him to take care of my Potaraka Island for me."

Once the Bodhisattva had subdued the black monster, she flew right back to the Southern Sea on a holy cloud. The Monkey King said goodbye to the Bodhisattva and rushed to the Black Wind Cave with the cassock. The small devils had already scattered in fright. Sun Wukong gathered some dry twigs, piled them around the cave, set them alight, and turned the Black Wind Cave into a Red Glow Cave.

Just when the Tang Priest was beginning to get anxious about Sun Wukong, he saw the Monkey King coming down from the air in some colourful clouds. "Master, I've got the cassock back," Monkey shouted. Xuanzang was delighted and all the monks said happily, "Good, good, now our lives are safe."

The next morning Master and disciple left the Guanyin Monastery, hurrying West. Of course, their journey was far from dull. If you want to know what adventures lay in store for them, read the explanation in the next instalment.